LIONS & TIGERS & BEARS ®

Publishing Incorporated

No part of this publication may be reproduced in whole or in part, or stored in a retrieval system, or transmitted in any form or by any means, electronic, mechanical, photocopying, recording, or otherwise, without written permission of the publisher.

ISBN 1-893459-01-2

Text and Illustrations copyright © 2001 by Dannel Roberts
All rights reserved.

Published by Lions & Tigers & Bears, Publishing Inc.

Come visit us at: MeAndUncleMike.com

Printed in the U.S.A.

Back when I was a kid one of my best friends was Uncle Mike. He was a little older than I was. We use to have a lot of fun doing things together. Once in a while we would go out into the hay field and practice sword fighting. We were the best sword fighters in the entire hay field. Now I'm going to tell you a story about the time Me and Uncle Mike had to use our sword fighting skills.

A long time ago in a city far, far away there was a big problem. The city was Boston, Massachusetts. The problem was that someone was a breaking into houses at night and stealing all the jewels throughout the whole city. They were stealing diamonds, emeralds, rubies, sapphires, silver, rings, necklaces, and anything made out of gold. Nobody knew who the thieves were.

People made sure their houses were locked at night. But even sure lock homes didn't solve the problem. First the people of Boston called in the police. Then they called in the sheriffs. Then they called in the marshals. Then they called in the FBI. Then they called in the CIA. But nobody could solve this mystery. Finally they called in M A U M. Do you know what that stands for?

That's right, it stands for Me and Uncle Mike. We got on our bikes and headed out. We took the long and winding road. It took a long time to get there. It was a regular marathon to get to Boston. They were so happy to see us they were going to throw us a tea party. But Uncle Mike said, "Cancel that tea party and show me the last place any clues were seen."

They took us down to a rough part of town. Then they showed us some strange looking footprints on the seashore. These were the only clues they had. Everybody else was scared and took off. Me and Uncle Mike weren't afraid. So we started looking around. We saw this guy sitting on a dock in the bay. He was a rough looking dude. He said, "Hey boys, come over here!"

We didn't know it but this guy was Shanghai Charlie. We walked over to him and he jumped up and grabbed us. He tied us up and put us in a couple of potato sacks. Then Shanghai Charlie dragged us off. He stopped at the end of a dock and tossed us into a rowboat. Next he rowed us out to sea. We had been shanghaied. That means they kidnap you and make you work on a pirate ship.

The rowboat came up along side a big old pirate ship. Shanghai Charlie finally dumped us out of those potato sacks. He told Me and Uncle Mike to get aboard. We climbed up over the side of that ship. There were some great big cannons on both sides. When we got on board, we saw a treasure chest. These were the thieves that were stealing all the gold and jewels from Boston.

The Pirate Captain came on deck and said three things. "If you try to escape we'll flog you." That means they take a cat with nine tails and whack you across the back. "If you try to escape again we'll keel-haul you." That means they tie a rope around you and haul you underneath the boat. "If you try to escape a third time we'll make you walk the plank and let the sharks eat you."

The Pirate Captain said that I was the new cabin boy. Next he said that Uncle Mike was going to be potato-peeling boy. He pointed his sword at us and said, "Get to work boys." Then he started shouting orders to his crew, "Pull the anchor", "Set the sails", and "Head East". Things looked pretty bad for Me and Uncle Mike because we were on a slow boat to China.

They worked us all day long. We had sailed so far that we couldn't see land anymore. They gave us a break to eat supper. After those pirates finished supper, they all drank rum until they all got dumb. Then they laid in a heap until they all went to sleep. Uncle Mike said this was our chance to escape. But there was one problem. The night watchman was Peg Leg Magilicutty.

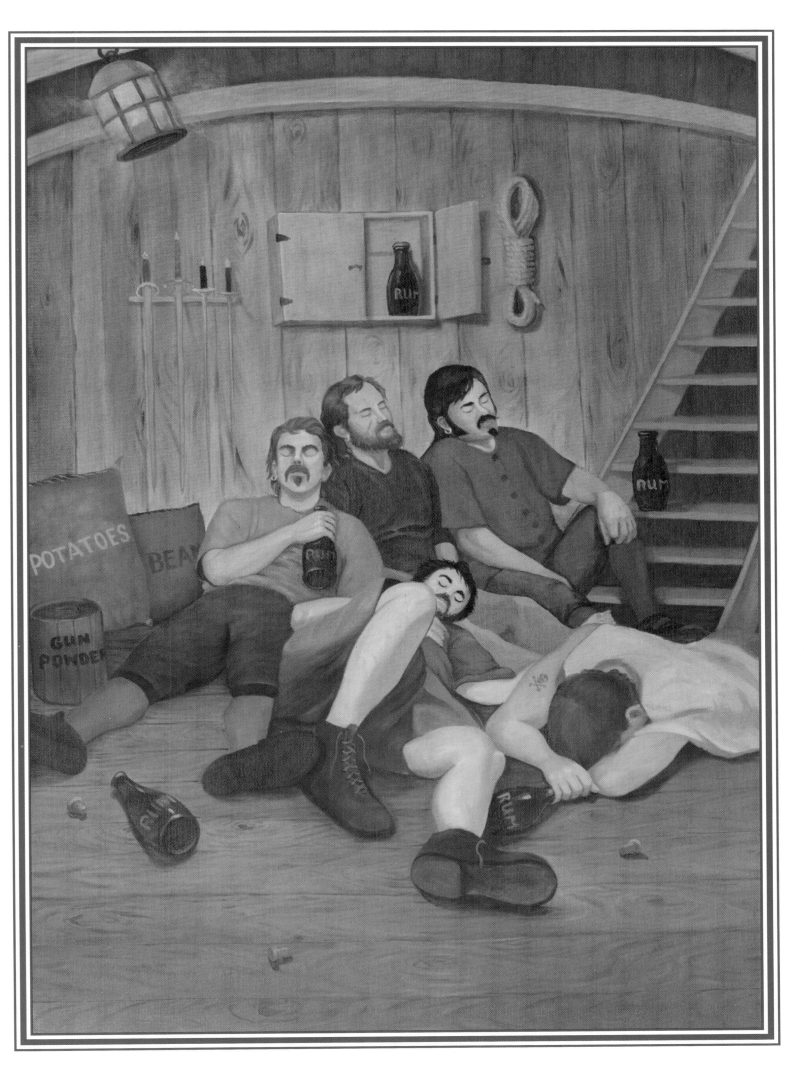

He was the best one legged sword fighter in the entire world. If we were going to take over the ship, someone had to challenge him to a sword fight. Uncle Mike said we could do rock, paper, scissors to see who would do the sword fighting. We did it. I had paper and Uncle Mike had rock. Uncle Mike said that rock mashes paper so I had to take on Peg Leg Magilicutty.

Uncle Mike took a cannon ball and climbed up into the crow's nest. I took a sword from a sleeping pirate and challenged Peg Leg Magilicutty. He pulled out his sword and came right after me. He was better than me. I acted fast and backed him underneath the crow's nest. Then Uncle Mike dropped that cannon ball on Peg Leg Magilicutty and knocked him colder than a three-dog night.

We had control of the ship. I took the helm and turned the ship around and headed home. Uncle Mike went below deck to get the treasure. He was down there a long time taking care of business. We sailed into some bad weather. We were riding the storm out. Then at daylight we came into Boston harbor. We dropped anchor, loaded the treasure chest in a rowboat and headed for shore.

Peg Leg Magilicutty's parrot ratted on us and woke everybody up. Pirates were everywhere on deck. We heard the Pirate Captain say, "Raise the anchor and bring the ship around for a broadside". Then he said, "Fire". Uncle Mike said, "Hold your ears". The whole ship exploded! There was smoke on the water and fire in the sky. All that was left of the ship was dust in the wind.

I thought we were done for. But it turned out that Uncle Mike had plugged up every cannon with beans and potatoes. That caused the ship to explode when they fired those cannons. We rowed to shore and gave the treasure back to the people of Boston. Potatoes and beans were blown all over the city. Those beans were baked and the potatoes got mashed.

They threw us a tea party. Of course, Me and Uncle Mike were even more famous. If you don't believe this story, then check any history book. Check to see where the Boston Tea Party came from. Check to see where Boston baked beans came from. Check to see if baked beans cause explosions. Check and see. Because it's like Grandpa always said, "Don't believe everything you hear".

About The Author

Dannel Roberts comes from a long line of storytellers. He was born in 1960 and raised in the state of Missouri. Dannel liked the outdoors, hunting, fishing, motorcycling, sports and the like. He later went on to graduate from Truman State University in 1982. Dannel met his wife, Martha, while in college. After they married, they moved to Central Missouri and had four children. Martha and Dannel bought hundreds of books for their children and spent many hours reading to them. One day Dannel was telling a "real" story about himself and his brother ("Uncle Mike"). Dannel's children liked these stories better than books. Then, to add some extra fun to these stories, Dannel started mixing in jokes, people, places and things that were out of character and out of context. His children loved this. Dannel continued telling these stories to his extended family, where he discovered adults loved the stories as well as children. With the encouragement of friends and family, Dannel now publishes his work.

About Uncle Mike

Uncle Mike is the author's older brother. His real name is Mike Roberts. The two brothers had many experiences they shared as they grew up together. Uncle Mike lives in Northern Missouri with his wife, Connie, and their three children. Uncle Mike has been a major force in getting the "Me and Uncle Mike" series published. He has helped with the editing, formatting, illustrating and promotion of the series. We have tried to make "Uncle Mike" that older brother that was always there when you needed him, even though he might have been the cause of the problem.

About The Illustrator

Frederick Thomas Stolte was born in 1946. He was raised in the Western Missouri area and started painting at the age of 14. He attributes his early interest in art to a grandmother who loved to paint in oils. Fred later moved to Central Missouri, where he married his wife Linda. They owned and operated an art store where Fred continued to paint portraits, nature scenes, still life, seascapes and various other commissioned works. After viewing Fred's work, Dannel and Uncle Mike commissioned him to do this book.

About The Models

The last illustration in the book, of the Boston Tea Party, presents the whole family. The author used his two sons as models for "Me and Uncle Mike". Elijah Ray Roberts (in red t-shirt) is "Me". Caleb Augustus Roberts (in white t-shirt) is "Uncle Mike". The author, Dannel Roberts, is in the center (with the "Mayor" ribbon). The two young girls are his daughters, Jessica Lynn (left) and Jilli Ann (right). The man (in blue) is the authors' brother Mike Roberts (the real "Uncle Mike") and the woman (in blue) is the authors' wife Martha Lynn. Pictured behind the author are Frederick Stolte (the illustrator) and his wife Linda, who worked with the books graphics, layout and cover design.

Come and see us at: MeAndUncleMike.com